3-Minute Take-Along Treas

FAIRY TALES

CONTENTS

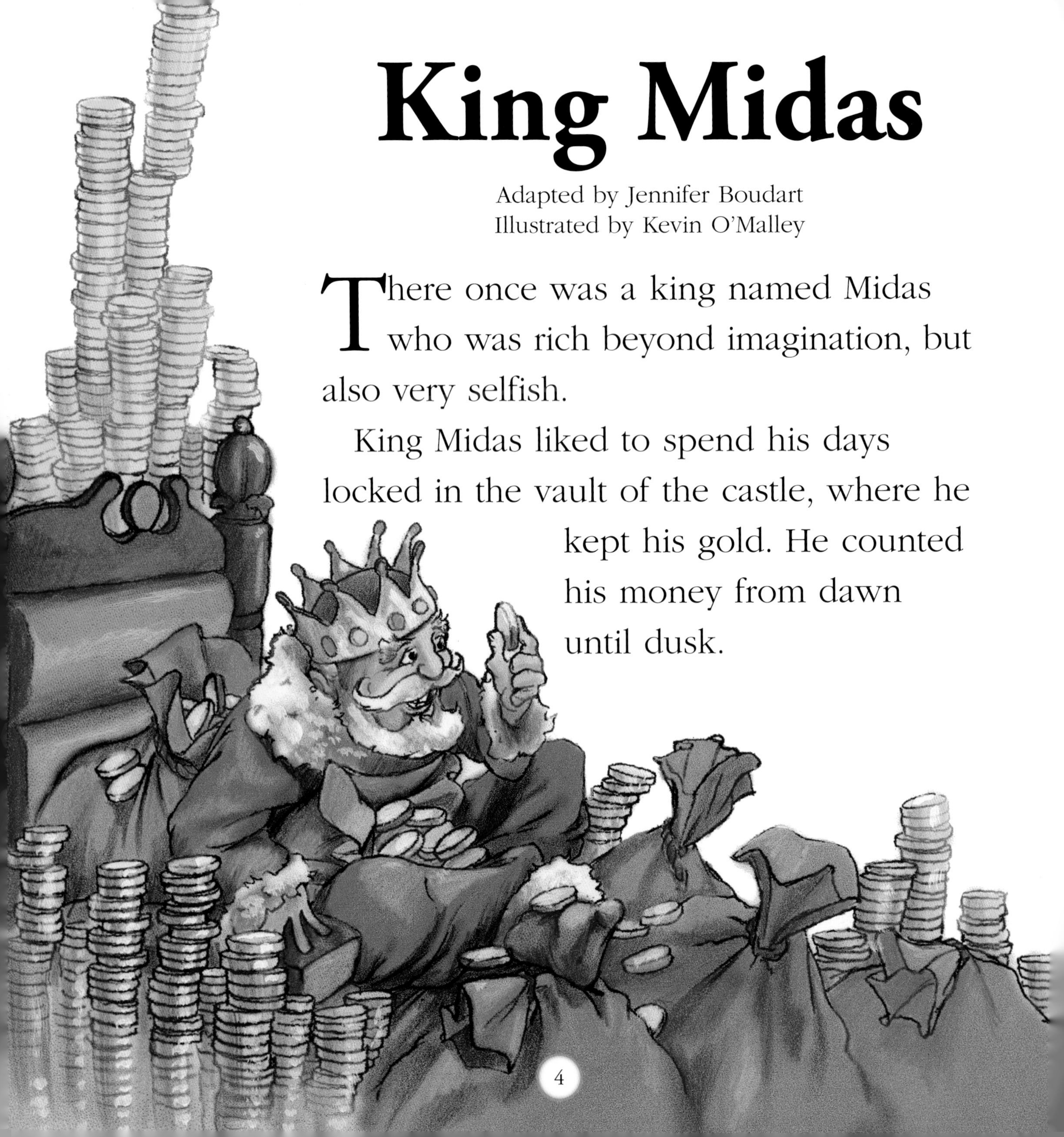

King Midas

Adapted by Jennifer Boudart
Illustrated by Kevin O'Malley

There once was a king named Midas who was rich beyond imagination, but also very selfish.

King Midas liked to spend his days locked in the vault of the castle, where he kept his gold. He counted his money from dawn until dusk.

King Midas had a daughter named Marygold, who liked to spend her days outdoors among the roses in the garden. There was nothing Marygold liked better than smelling their sweet scent.

One morning, Marygold said, “Father, won’t you join me in the garden today?”

“Oh no, Marygold,” King Midas replied. “There is so much gold to count. I really must go down to the vault right away.”

This saddened Marygold. She was certain that her father would enjoy her roses if he ever saw them in full bloom.

Later that day, a mysterious stranger appeared in the vault.

"Good afternoon, Your Majesty," said the stranger.

"How did you get in here?" asked King Midas angrily.

"Nevermind that," said the stranger. "I have come to offer you the power to turn all that you touch into gold."

"I would like that very much indeed!" said the greedy Midas.

"Very well," said the stranger. "After the next sunrise, anything you touch will turn to gold." With that, the stranger disappeared.

As promised, King Midas awoke the next morning with a magical touch. He ran from room to room, turning things into solid gold.

King Midas rushed outside to Marygold's garden. He touched a rose and it turned from scarlet red to golden yellow.

"How delighted Marygold will be," Midas said, "when she finds I have turned all her flowers into precious gold."

Soon the king's stomach began to rumble.

Changing things to gold had made Midas very hungry. He returned to the castle to have breakfast. But as soon as Midas touched his food and drink, it turned to gold.

Suddenly, Marygold came into the room, holding a golden rose.

"My precious roses are ruined!" sobbed Marygold.

Without thinking, the king rushed over to give his daughter a comforting hug.

As soon as King Midas touched her, Marygold turned into solid gold!

King Midas was shocked at what he had done. He now knew that his magic touch was a curse, not a blessing. How could he have been so greedy?

Just then, the mysterious stranger returned and asked, "Aren't you pleased with all your gold, King Midas?"

"I don't care about gold anymore," answered Midas. "I just want Marygold back."

"I see you have learned a lesson," said the stranger. "To get your daughter back, go dive into the river. Bring back enough water to sprinkle over the things you have turned to gold, and they will return to normal."

Midas and his servants ran to the river. Midas leaped into the water. The servants quickly filled their buckets before all the water completely changed to gold.

Back at the castle, King Midas splashed water over Marygold. She instantly turned back into herself.

Together, Midas and Marygold went outside and changed all the golden flowers back into beautiful red roses.

"I promise never to waste any more days counting my gold," King Midas said, giving Marygold another hug.

Finally, King Midas had learned that there are more important things in life than gold.

Thumbelina

Adapted by Lynne Suesse
Illustrated by Jane Maday

Once there was a kind woman who lived all alone in the woods. She felt lucky to be surrounded by the beauty of nature. Her only wish was for a child to share her joy.

One day, a kind old witch passed by. "I know you want a child more than anything," said the witch. "I can help you."

The witch pulled a tiny bag out of her cloak.

"This magic tulip bulb will make your wish come true!" she said.

The woman planted the bulb at once. Within moments, a beautiful flower popped out of the soil.

When the woman sniffed the delicate blossom, the petals burst open. Sitting in the center of the flower was a beautiful little child.

"Why, you are no bigger than my thumb! I will call you Thumbelina." The woman knew she would love the little girl as her own.

One day, a toad heard Thumbelina singing a sweet song. The toad decided that Thumbelina should marry her son. The toad stole Thumbelina and placed her on a lily pad in the middle of a stream.

"Stay here while I get my son," demanded the toad as she dove under the water.

"Oh, I don't want to be a toad's wife!" wailed Thumbelina.

As she cried, three fish swam by and took pity on Thumbelina. They nibbled at the stem of the lily pad until it broke free.

Thumbelina sailed swiftly down the stream, and soon she reached the bank. She was tired from her adventure. A butterfly helped her weave blades of grass into a sturdy hammock.

Another butterfly carried a leaf up to make a pillow for Thumbelina's pretty head.

Thumbelina missed her mother very much, but she could not find her way home.

Soon the weather began to get cold. Thumbelina knew she had to find a warm place to live. Luckily, she met a friendly mouse who invited Thumbelina to stay.

One day, Thumbelina and the mouse heard a strange noise. It was a sparrow who had hurt his wing and could not fly. They invited him inside.

The sparrow was surprised to see such a tiny person.

"Are you a fairy?" asked the sparrow.

"What is a fairy?" asked Thumbelina.

"When my wing is better, I will show you," said the sparrow.

That winter, while the mouse sewed and the sparrow rested, Thumbelina sang to pass the time. The mouse and the sparrow even made her a singing stage from a thimble the mouse had found outside her house.

When spring arrived, the sparrow's wing felt as good as new. He offered to take Thumbelina home to her mother. Thumbelina and the sparrow thanked the mouse for her kindness, and they flew away.

Soon the sparrow landed in an enchanted grove.

"This isn't where I live," said Thumbelina, confused.

Just then, a tiny boy stepped out from the petals of a big white flower. He was the prince of the fairies!

The prince took one look at Thumbelina and knew he must have her for his bride.

"I will marry you," said Thumbelina, "if you come and live in my mother's garden. I miss her so!"

The sparrow took the tiny prince and princess to the woman's garden. The woman was thrilled to find not only her beloved daughter, but also a new little son-in-law!

The sparrow visited every summer, and they all lived happily ever after.

The Wild Swans

Adapted by Brian Conway
Illustrated by Kathy Mitchell

Once there was a king who had three fine sons and a sweet daughter named Elise. One day, the king hurried to Elise with terrible news.

"Your brothers have been taken away from us," he told her. "I know not where. I cannot stand to lose you, too."

The king told Elise to go with his most trusted servants, who would take her to the safety of their home in the forest.

Elise lived hidden away for many years. When she was old enough, she set off in search of her brothers. She had no idea where to look, but she knew in her heart they were still alive, and something inside told her they needed her help.

After several days of wandering and searching, Elise met an old woman.

“Have you seen three princes?” asked Elise.

“No, but I have seen three white swans with golden crowns on their heads,” the old woman replied. She showed Elise where she had seen them.

Just then, as the sun was setting, Elise looked up to see three majestic swans. They landed beside her and changed magically into three princes. Elise was overjoyed to see her brothers. They told her that an evil sorcerer had cast a spell that turned them into swans during the day. At nightfall, the moonlight made them human again. The sorcerer had also imprisoned their dear father. Elise had escaped to safety just in time.

Elise promised to do whatever she could to break the sorcerer’s wicked spell. And they all vowed to find their father and free him, too.

That night, a fairy came to Elise in a dream. "Only you can free your brothers," the fairy whispered. "But you must sacrifice greatly."

"You must craft three shirts from the petals of roses," continued the fairy. "When you cover the swans with these shirts, the spell will be broken. But you must not open your mouth to eat, drink, or speak until the shirts are made. If you do, your brothers will be swans forever."

Elise awoke with a start to find the cave in which she slept was surrounded with hundreds of lovely rosebushes. She set to work immediately.

Elise worked day and night for thirty days. Her brothers visited her at the cave each night, and searched for their father during the day.

Elise didn't dare speak to tell them what she was doing. They cried for her pain and understood that she worked to help them.

At long last, weak and starved, Elise completed the third shirt. With barely the energy to lift even one rose petal, she summoned her last bit of strength to drape the shirts over her swan brothers. Before her eyes, the swans became men again. Elise fell into her brothers' arms and, in a faint voice, explained how the spell had been broken.

"Now if only we had Father back," she whispered.

What the dream-fairy had not told Elise was that her sacrifice was powerful enough to rob the sorcerer of all his power. The sorcerer's evil could not withstand a love as great as Elise's—a love so great that she had risked her own life to save her brothers. Their father was instantly freed!

Once reunited, the happy family thrived again, and never parted from one another for the rest of their days.

The Emperor's New Clothes

Adapted by Mary Rowitz
Illustrated by John Kanzler

Once upon a time, there was a vain emperor who loved clothes more than anything else. The emperor's clothes filled all the closets and rooms in the royal palace.

The emperor also spent a lot of money on mirrors. He thought his fancy clothes made him look quite dashing, so he spent most of his free time looking at himself.

Word of the emperor who loved fine clothes reached two thieves in a faraway land. The clever thieves thought of a plan.

The thieves dressed up as traveling tailors and journeyed to the emperor's palace. They told the palace guards that they had rare and wonderful fabrics to show the emperor.

The thieves were welcomed and taken straight into the throne room.

The thieves told the emperor that their magical fabric was invisible to fools.

Then the thieves opened their bag and pretended to lift something out.

The emperor squinted. He saw nothing at all! *I must be a fool!* he thought. The emperor was very embarrassed, so he said, "That fabric is magnificent! I will offer you twenty pieces of gold to make me a suit with it."

The thieves, delighted, took the emperor's measurements and got to work.

After a few days, the royal minister went to see how the suit was coming along. He found the tailors cutting away at the air with their scissors and sewing up fabric that was not there!

I cannot see any fabric! Could it be that I am a fool? gulped the minister.

"Say, minister," said a thief, "order us some more food, would you? All this hard work makes us hungry."

That much must be true, the minister thought. *The tailors had eaten so much already. They must be working hard on something!*

The minister hurried off to report back to the emperor.

"Your Majesty, the tailors are hard at work on your suit," he said. The minister did not want to appear foolish, so he added, "It is simply divine!"

At long last, the thieves brought the emperor his new suit, and he put it on.

The emperor stood in front of a mirror, wearing only his underwear and admiring a new suit that wasn't even there!

The emperor called for a royal parade the next day. He wanted to show off his new suit to everyone in the land.

At the parade, everyone pushed and shoved to get the best view. The people had heard that fools could not see the magical fabric, and they wanted to find out who amongst them was a fool.

No one would admit that they couldn't see the emperor's suit. Nobody wanted to look like a fool.

Suddenly a boy cried out, "The emperor is wearing nothing but his underwear!"

Everyone in the crowd began to laugh. They had all been foolish. They pretended to see a suit that was not even there, because they were afraid of what others would think.

The embarrassed emperor rushed back to the palace to put on some clothes.

Then he invited the honest boy to speak with him. "I hereby proclaim you a junior minister," said the emperor. "You have proven your courage and bravery by telling the truth when no one else would!"

The Goose Girl

Adapted by Lisa Harkrader
Illustrated by Cindy Salans Rosenheim

Once a graceful, kind princess named Elizabeth promised to marry a prince she had never met. Elizabeth watched as her belongings were loaded onto her beloved horse, Falada. Falada was a special horse, for he could speak.

The princess's mother, a kind and generous queen, chose a servant named Zelda to look after the princess. Then the queen gave Elizabeth one last gift.

"This is my royal ring," said the queen. "I want you to have it. When you arrive at your new castle, this ring will prove who you are."

Princess Elizabeth and Zelda set off for the prince's kingdom. Elizabeth rode faithful Falada, and Zelda rode a sure-footed old mare.

After a few miles, Princess Elizabeth grew thirsty. She knelt on the bank of a stream to drink. As she drank, her mother's ring slid from her finger, but Elizabeth did not notice. Zelda waded into the stream and fetched it.

Elizabeth was brushing the mud from her gown when she saw the ring was gone. "Oh, no!" she cried.

Zelda held up the ring. "Is this what you're looking for, Princess?"

"Thank goodness! Zelda, you've saved me," said a grateful Elizabeth.

"This time, perhaps." Zelda slid the ring onto her own finger. "But what about next time? I should keep this for you. And after what just happened, I think I should ride Falada and keep an eye on your possessions."

"You're right," said the princess. "You're too good to me."

After switching clothes and horses, Elizabeth and Zelda set off once more.

At the castle, the king was waiting.

"Show me to my room and send up some food," said Zelda. "I'm tired and hungry."

The king was surprised at Zelda's rudeness, but he said politely, "We are delighted that you've arrived safely, Princess." He turned to Elizabeth. "We'll find a room for you and send you a hot meal."

"Thank you, Your Majesty," said Elizabeth. "But I'm the princess."

Zelda snorted. "You? Your clothes are rags and you were riding a swayback mare." Zelda held out her hand to show off the queen's ring. "This proves who I am. My mother gave it to me before we left."

The king sent Elizabeth off with the goose boy, Conrad. She was to be the new goose girl.

Each morning, Elizabeth and Conrad led the geese to a meadow. One day, Elizabeth found Falada in a pasture in the farthest corner of the kingdom.

The two old friends talked and talked. Elizabeth insisted that she and Conrad take the geese to Falada's pasture each day. Conrad grew tired of walking so far, and went to complain to the king.

"She talks to that horse all day," said Conrad, "and the horse just tells her that a princess should not be tending geese." Curious, the king went to the pasture. The talking horse revealed that Elizabeth was indeed the true princess!

That very night, the king declared that Zelda would be the goose girl from then on. He now knew that he should have recognized a true princess by her goodness and grace, not by her fine clothes and jewels.

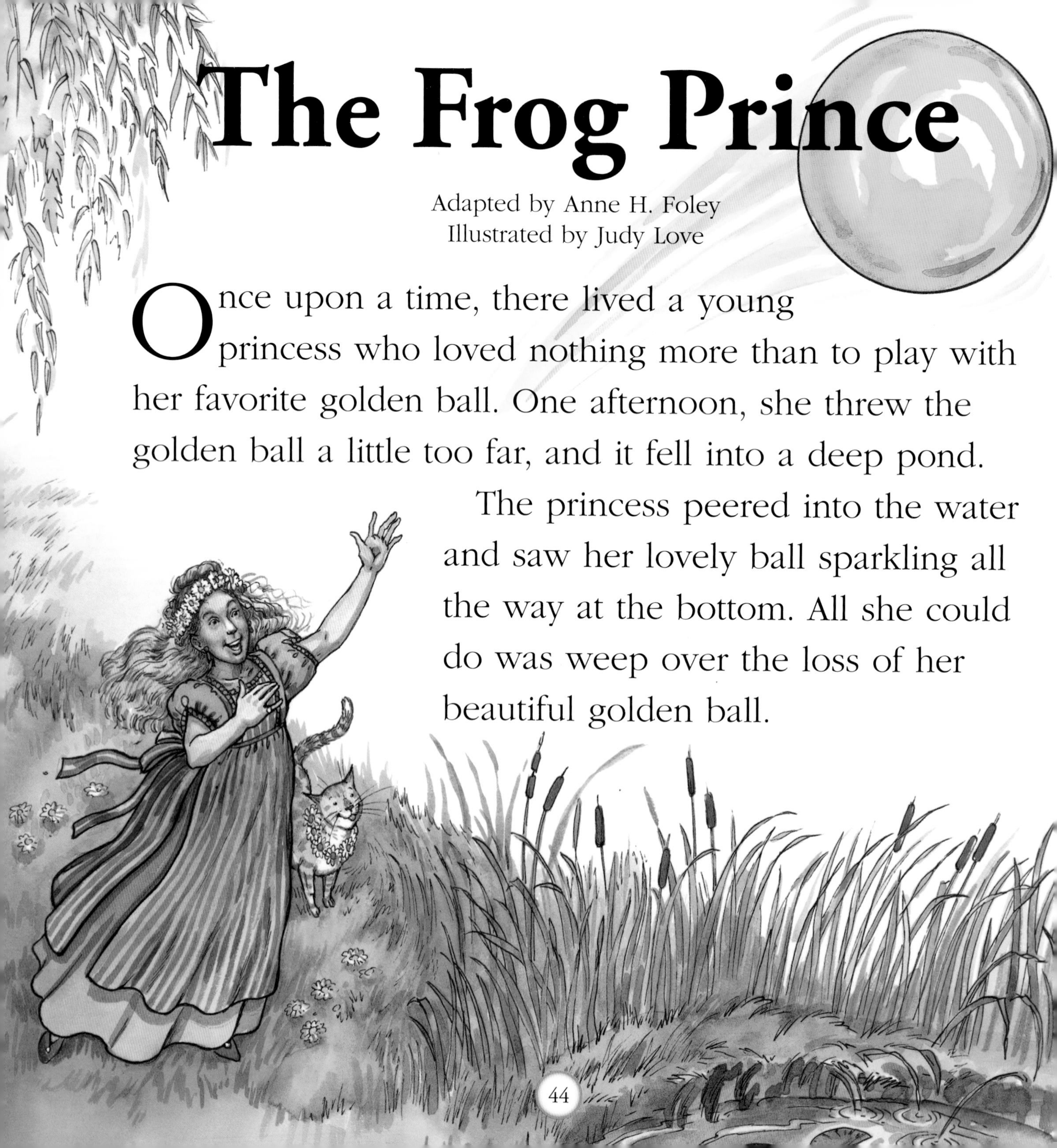

The Frog Prince

Adapted by Anne H. Foley
Illustrated by Judy Love

Once upon a time, there lived a young princess who loved nothing more than to play with her favorite golden ball. One afternoon, she threw the golden ball a little too far, and it fell into a deep pond.

The princess peered into the water and saw her lovely ball sparkling all the way at the bottom. All she could do was weep over the loss of her beautiful golden ball.

Suddenly, the princess heard a voice say, "What troubles you?"

The princess looked down and saw a frog. The princess had never seen a talking frog before, but she hid her surprise and answered him.

"I am crying because my golden ball is lost in the pond," she said.

The frog said, "I will rescue your golden ball, if you promise you will be my friend forever."

The princess did not want to befriend a slimy frog! She hoped he would forget his request as soon as the task was done.

"I promise," lied the princess, "that we shall be best friends."

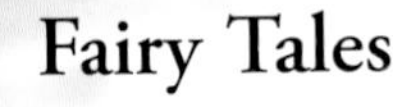

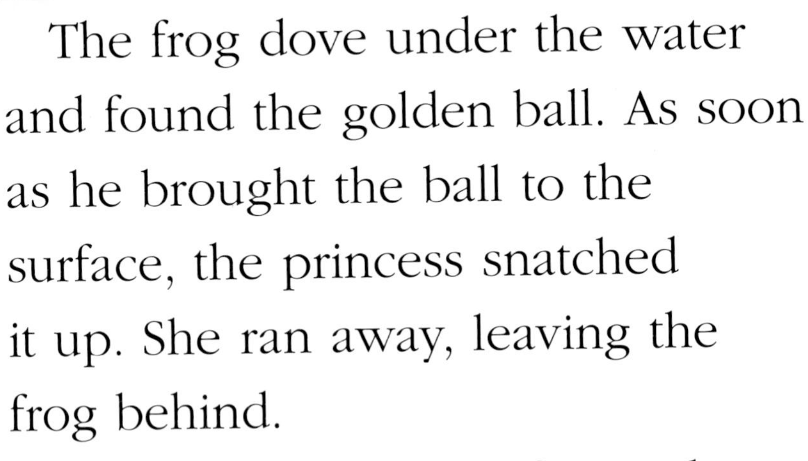

The frog dove under the water and found the golden ball. As soon as he brought the ball to the surface, the princess snatched it up. She ran away, leaving the frog behind.

But the frog did not forget the princess's promise. That evening, the frog hopped all the way to the castle, and hopped into the dining hall as the royal family was eating dinner.

"*Mmmm,* I love mashed potatoes and peas!" he exclaimed, as he began to eat from the princess's plate.

"*Er,* Princess," said the king, "why is there a frog at the dinner table?"

The princess explained the promise she had made, looking at the frog with disgust all the while.

"Whether you like the frog or not," said the stern king, "you must keep your promise to him."

Reluctantly, the princess offered her friendship—and her dinner—to the frog.

"Now I am thirsty," croaked the frog. "Water, please, Princess."

The princess remembered her promise to the frog. She poured him a glass of water, and he drank it down.

"Now for dessert! I'd like some shoofly pie," said the frog.

The princess could take no more of the frog's demands. She slammed her fist on the table. The table shook, and the frog lost his balance and fell off the table. The princess and the king leaned over the edge of the table to see what had happened to the frog. But instead of the frog, there was a handsome young prince!

"What is going on here?" asked the furious princess.

The prince explained, "An evil witch turned me into a frog. The only way I could become a prince again was to make a princess angry with me. When you appeared, I saw a chance to break the spell. Your anger has turned me back into a prince! You have saved my life."

In that brief moment, the princess and the prince fell in love and were soon married. The princess forgave the prince for deceiving her, and the prince forgave the princess for trying to break her promise.

The two agreed to be honest with one another forever more, and the joyous couple spent the rest of their days together.

Hansel and Gretel

Adapted by Brian Conway
Illustrated by Thea Kliros

In a tiny cottage at the edge of the forest, there lived a poor woodcutter and his two dear children, Hansel and Gretel.

One day, the woodcutter called his children into the house.

"Our cupboards are empty," he sighed. "Though I work hard every day, I still do not have enough to feed myself and both of you children."

"I'm afraid I must teach you how to care for yourselves," he continued, sadly. "Tomorrow I will teach you how to hunt, fish, and gather fruit."

Hansel and Gretel were clever children who wanted to make their father proud. So they made a plan to help him.

Early the next morning, the children set out into the woods without their father, hoping to bring back enough food for supper.

Hansel and Gretel dropped a trail of bread crumbs behind them as they walked. They planned to follow the trail back home.

They wandered through the woods all day long, but could find no food. Too late, the children discovered that their path of bread crumbs had been eaten up by birds. They were lost!

Suddenly, they saw a lonely little house. As they got closer, they could not believe their eyes. It was a gingerbread house, covered with sweets! The children broke pieces from the house and began to eat them.

Just then, the door opened and an old woman hobbled out.

"Please excuse us," said Hansel. "But we are lost and very hungry."

"Well, well," said the old woman, peering down at the children. "Come inside and I will fix you a nice hot meal."

Hansel and Gretel followed the woman into the house. Immediately, the old woman served them hot turkey, fresh fruit, cookies, and cakes. The children ate and ate.

"Go ahead," said the woman. "Have some more."

Hansel and Gretel happily filled their plates again. The old woman held Gretel's arm and said, "My, but you are skinny. I will fatten you right up!"

Startled, Gretel said, "But I like the size I am now! Why should I be fatter?"

"All children should be plump and healthy," said the old woman with a chuckle. "I hope you two have room for some apple pie!"

Hansel and Gretel wondered why the old woman had not eaten. She kept busy in the kitchen, building up the fire in the oven.

"There is just one more dish to make," she said with a scary laugh. "I will have my fill of it soon."

"I think this strange old woman is not nice at all!" whispered Hansel, worried.

"She wants us to be plump so she can put us in that oven and have us for supper!" said Gretel.

Hansel and Gretel snuck up behind the old woman, bumped her into the oven, and ran away as fast as they could!

After many days of searching, Hansel and Gretel found their way back to their father's cottage. As soon as the woodcutter saw his children, he ran to hug them.

"I've missed you both so much," he said. "I promise we'll always have enough to eat, and I will never let you out of my sight again."

Hansel and Gretel were happy to be home.

Cinderella

Adapted by Amy Adair
Illustrated by Kathi McCord

Once upon a time, there was a sweet, kind, and pretty young girl named Cinderella. She had a very mean stepmother and two stepsisters who made her life miserable. They all treated Cinderella as if she were a mere servant.

Cinderella worked hard all day while her stepmother and stepsisters spent their days preening in front of the mirror. But her heart was so pure, she didn't even mind.

One day, something very exciting arrived. It was an invitation to the prince's fancy ball! But Cinderella was not allowed to go.

Finally, it was the night of the ball. As the stepmother and her daughters climbed into their coach and rode off to the ball, Cinderella began to cry to herself. "Why must I stay at home and sweep up the hearth while everyone else goes to the ball? Am I not as good and kind as everyone else?"

Suddenly, Cinderella's fairy godmother magically appeared!

"Do not cry," the fairy said, sweetly. "Tonight you shall go to the ball."

Cinderella was so happy she thought she would burst. Then she was sad again. "How will I get there? What will I wear?"

With a wave of her wand, the fairy godmother turned an ordinary pumpkin into a lavish coach. *Poof!* The fairy godmother transformed six white mice into strong white horses, and changed a rat into a handsome driver.

Finally, the fairy godmother waved her wand, and Cinderella's old dress turned into a lovely gown, complete with delicate glass slippers.

As Cinderella stepped into her coach, her fairy godmother called out a warning. "At midnight, the coach will turn back into a pumpkin, the horses into mice, the driver into a rat. You must not be late!" she said.

When Cinderella arrived at the ball, the prince fell in love with her at first sight. He would dance with no one else. As they glided across the floor, Cinderella fell in love with the prince, too.

Cinderella was so happy, she forgot the time. When the clock sounded the ninth stroke of midnight, Cinderella remembered her fairy godmother's warning and dashed out of the ballroom!

Cinderella flew down the palace steps in such a hurry, she left one of her glass slippers behind.

The prince ran after Cinderella, but it was too late. She was already gone. He had never even learned her name!

The prince spied the glass slipper on the palace steps. *It must belong to her*, he thought. He vowed to find the slipper's mysterious owner.

The very next day, the prince began to search for the maiden who fit into the glass slipper. He visited every home in the land. Finally, the prince arrived at Cinderella's house.

The stepsisters both tried on the slipper. They pulled and tugged and pushed, but their feet were just too big.

Cinderella asked softly, "May I try?"

The prince held out the glass slipper for Cinderella. Her foot slipped into it with ease!

"It fits!" shrieked the stepmother.

"It fits!" howled the stepsisters.

"It fits!" whispered the prince.

He was so overcome with love and joy that he and Cinderella were married that very day! They lived happily ever after.

As for the stepmother and stepsisters, Cinderella did not punish them. But they did have to learn how to do their own cooking, cleaning, and ironing. And that was punishment enough.

The Twelve Dancing Princesses

Adapted by Sarah Toast
Illustrated by Pamela R. Levy

Long ago, there lived a king and his twelve beautiful daughters. The princesses all slept in one huge bedroom. Even though the king carefully locked their door each night, the princesses were tired and out of sorts every morning. More puzzling still, their silk slippers were worn to shreds.

Determined to find out the truth, the king issued a proclamation declaring that whoever solved the mystery of where the twelve princesses went to dance every night, could choose a wife from among them. However, if the suitor failed to discover the secret within three days and nights, he would be banished from the kingdom forever.

Then one day, a poor soldier came limping along the road. He had heard about the proclamation, and he wanted to try to marry a princess. He had stopped to rest and eat when an old beggar woman shuffled by.

He did not have much food, but he offered to share with the woman nevertheless.

"You have shown me great kindness," said the woman. "To repay you, I will tell you this: do not drink the wine the princesses offer you. Pretend to fall asleep. And take this cloak, which will make you invisible. Follow the princesses to learn their secret!"

The soldier arrived at the castle that evening and was led to the little room next to the princesses'. Soon the eldest princess brought the soldier a cup of wine. He pretended to drink it, letting it trickle down his chin and onto his scarf. Then he pretended to fall asleep.

Soon the twelve princesses put on their new silk slippers. Then the eldest princess tapped on her bedpost three times. The bed descended into the floor and became a flight of stairs. The soldier threw on the cloak and followed them down the stairway.

Eventually, they came to a forest of gold, silver, and diamond trees. As the princesses hurried through, the soldier reached up and broke off a branch from each so he would have a way to prove his story.

At the edge of a lake, twelve princes in boats awaited the princesses. The princes rowed them across the lake to a castle, where the princesses danced the night away. The invisible soldier sneaked into a boat and went, too.

Hours later, they hurried back the way they had come. The soldier was able to dash ahead, throw off his cloak, and jump into bed. The princesses never knew they had been followed.

The next morning, the king sent for the soldier and asked him, “Have you discovered where my daughters dance their shoes to shreds every night?”

“Your Highness, I have,” said the soldier. “They go down a hidden staircase. Then they walk through an enchanted forest to a beautiful lake. Twelve princes take them across the lake to a castle where they dance all night.”

The king couldn’t believe the soldier’s story until the soldier showed him the branches of silver, gold, and diamonds. Then the king summoned his daughters, who at last admitted the truth.

The king told the soldier that he could choose one of the princesses to be his wife.

The soldier was given royal chambers and royal garments to wear. He and the eldest princess were married, and the wedding guests happily danced the night away.

Sleeping Beauty

Adapted by Brian Conway
Illustrated by Holly Jones

One happy day, a queen gave birth to a daughter. The entire kingdom celebrated the baby's arrival.

A very lonely, very wicked witch heard the news. She was terribly jealous of the queen's happiness, and crept into the castle to cast an evil spell on the baby.

Before she left, the witch stooped to whisper into the baby's ear. "When you reach the age of sixteen, you will have a simple sewing accident."

"You will prick your finger and fall into a deep sleep… and never awaken!" cackled the witch.

Years later, the princess's sixteenth birthday arrived. As the princess put on a dress for her party, she noticed it was torn. She found a needle and thread and began to mend the dress.

As she stitched, the princess pricked her finger. She fell to the floor in a deep sleep.

When the queen found her daughter, she called out to her and shook her shoulders. But the princess would not awaken.

Doctors from all over the kingdom were summoned to help the princess.

"This is magic," they said. "There is nothing we can do."

The queen called on all the wizards, witches, and warlocks in the land, but they could not break the spell either.

One day, a good fairy arrived with news for the queen. This fairy had met a wicked witch who had bragged about her powerful sleeping spell.

"But there is one thing that would break the spell: Love," said the fairy. "If a man of pure heart were to fall in love with her, she would awaken."

The kind fairy fluttered her wings and hovered by the sleeping girl's ear, whispering words of comfort to the princess.

"What man could fall in love with a sleeping girl?" sobbed the queen. "All hope is surely lost!"

"I cannot awaken your daughter," said the fairy, "but I can make you, and everyone in your castle, fall asleep until the day she wakes. Then you will not have to wait in sorrow."

The queen agreed. The fairy cast her spell, and all the people in the castle fell into a deep sleep.

One hundred years passed. A dense, dark forest grew around the silent castle.

One day, a young prince, who was exploring the forest, came upon a heavy stone wall buried beneath thick moss and vines.

"A hidden castle!" he said, excitedly.

While pushing open the creaky door, the prince tripped over something. He looked down and saw a palace guard sleeping peacefully. With every step he took inside the castle, he found more sleeping people.

Soon the prince came to the room where the princess lay in her deep sleep.

"A sleeping beauty," he whispered in awe. Overcome with emotion, the prince lifted her soft white hand and gently kissed it.

At that kiss, the princess's eyes opened in a flash.

"You have come to me at last!" she said. "I was waiting for you in my dream. A kind fairy told me you would come!"

At the same moment, the queen and her sleeping subjects awoke, too.

"The princess is awake at last!" they cheered.

"This prince has saved us," said the princess, with love and gratitude shining in her eyes.

In a few short days, the prince and princess were married. The princess had truly found the man of her dreams, and they lived happily ever after.

George and the Dragon

Adapted by Brian Conway
Illustrated by Tammie Speer Lyon

Once upon a time, there lived a boy named George. The queen of fairies had taken him in as a baby, and the fairies raised him as their own. They taught him to be a brave and noble knight.

At last the time came when George was old enough to seek out his destiny. The queen of fairies called him to see her.

"Your journey starts today," she told him. "You have many adventures before you now."

"Yes, Your Majesty." George bowed before the queen. He was sad to leave the land of the fairies, but he was not afraid.

In his travels, George heard countless stories of the hardship that had befallen the kingdom of Silene. George decided that was where he was needed most, and headed on his way.

When George reached Silene, he found that a high wall enclosed the castle and the small city around it. He saw no one at all, except for a young lady who had rushed out to meet him.

"You would do well to leave here now and never return," said the lady.

"But I have come to help you," George replied, "even if it costs me my life."

"Very well. I am Princess Sabra," she said. The princess told George why the kingdom lived in fear. A dragon had slain their king, and kept the villagers captive inside the city walls. The dragon demanded that he be given two sheep to eat each day, or he would eat the people for his dinner!

"We gave up our last two sheep this morning. Tomorrow we shall have nothing to give the dragon, and we shall all perish. What's more," she went on, "the dragon cannot be killed by sword alone. His scales are tougher than steel. Many have already died trying to defeat him."

Suddenly, George remembered a gift the fairy queen had given him. It was an hourglass filled with tiny blue grains of sand that looked as cold as ice. The hourglass bore an inscription, which read: *There is one way to save the rest: the Serpent's weakness is in his breath.*

George and Sabra hurried to the dragon's lair. "The time left in the hourglass will lead us," George whispered. "We must wait until all the sand has dropped through then we will know what to do."

George and Sabra arrived at the dragon's lair just as the dragon awoke from a deep slumber. As the dragon stretched and yawned a great, fiery yawn, the very last tiny blue grain of sand dropped through the hourglass.

George knew what must be done. He threw the hourglass at the dragon's yawning mouth. It shattered into a cloud of icy mist on the dragon's tongue.

The magical hourglass, which had actually contained crystals of frozen time, instantly froze the dragon's mouth shut! He had to live the rest of his days deep beneath the warm waters of a nearby lake, so that he would not freeze from the inside out.

George had saved the kingdom. In her gratitude, Sabra offered George all the riches she possessed. But George wanted no payment for his deeds. "I have many more adventures left to face," George told Sabra. "They are my greatest reward."

The Little Mermaid

Adapted by Lynne Suesse
Illustrated by Pamela R. Levy

Deep below the ocean waves, there was once a kingdom of mermaids and mermen. Here lived a family with six beautiful daughters. Each daughter looked forward to her eighteenth birthday, when she would be allowed to swim to the surface for her first look at the sky.

When it was the littlest mermaid's eighteenth birthday, she rushed up to peek above the waves. It was even more beautiful than she had imagined!

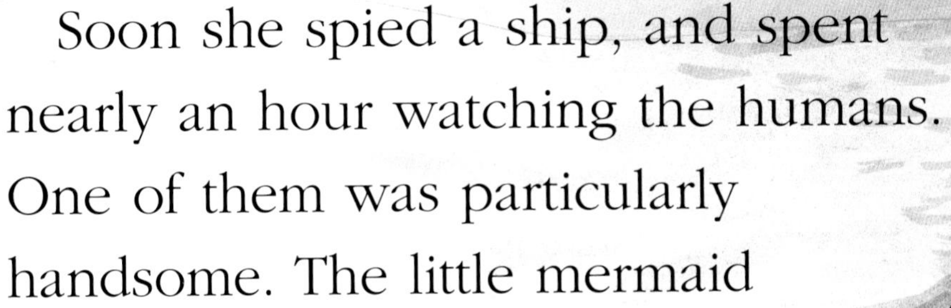

Soon she spied a ship, and spent nearly an hour watching the humans. One of them was particularly handsome. The little mermaid realized he must be a prince.

Suddenly, a terrible storm began. The prince's ship was torn to pieces by the pounding waves.

The little mermaid knew the prince could not live in the water, and took him safely to shore. The little mermaid brushed the hair from the prince's face and looked into his eyes, but became frightened and quickly swam away.

Back under the ocean, the little mermaid told her sisters about the handsome prince. As she told her story, she realized that she could not live without him.

That night, the little mermaid snuck away to see the sea witch. She knew the sea witch could give her what she wanted most.

The sea witch told the little mermaid that she would be happy to give her the legs she longed for, but there was a price for such a special gift: her voice.

She would be able to walk and dance, but unable to speak or sing.

The little mermaid agreed to the sea witch's demand, and swam to the surface to drink the magic potion. For a moment, she felt very strange. When she looked down, she saw that her tail had become two beautiful human legs!

On his morning walk, the prince discovered the beautiful girl on the beach. He asked her who she was and where she came from, but she could make no sound. The prince wrapped his cloak around the little mermaid, and took her back to the castle.

The prince was enchanted by this lovely girl. He felt that he had met her somewhere before. The two spent every moment together, taking long walks and gazing into each other's eyes. Even though the princess never uttered a word, the prince fell deeply in love.

Finally one day, the prince announced to his parents, the king and queen, that he planned to marry this beautiful, silent girl. But the king and queen forbade it! They wanted the prince to marry a princess, not a mysterious stranger. But when they saw the light of true love shining in their son's eyes, they gave their consent.

On the happiest day of the little mermaid's life, she and the handsome prince were married.

The best part of all was that the power of the prince's love overcame the sea witch's spell! The little mermaid kept her legs, and the moment they were married, she also regained her voice.

The first words spoken by the new princess were: "I do."

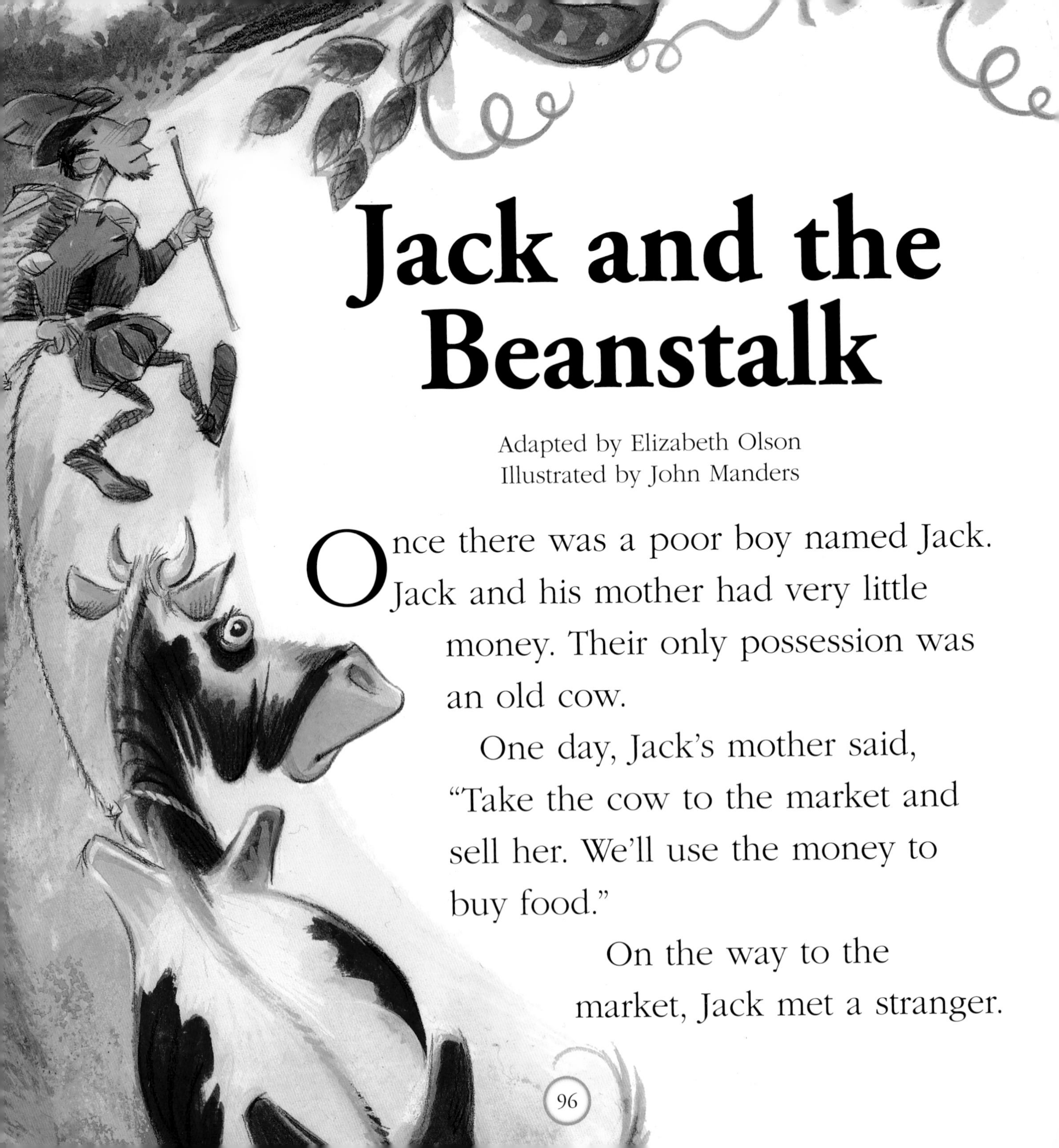

Jack and the Beanstalk

Adapted by Elizabeth Olson
Illustrated by John Manders

Once there was a poor boy named Jack. Jack and his mother had very little money. Their only possession was an old cow.

One day, Jack's mother said, "Take the cow to the market and sell her. We'll use the money to buy food."

On the way to the market, Jack met a stranger.

“I’ll give you five magic beans for that old cow,” offered the stranger.

Jack accepted the deal at once, and ran straight home to tell his mother the news.

“What have you done?” she shouted. “We can’t buy food with magic beans.”

She threw the beans out the window, and sent Jack to bed.

The next morning, Jack awoke to find that a beanstalk had grown from the magic beans! It reached all the way to the clouds.

Jack climbed up the beanstalk until he found himself above the clouds. To Jack's surprise, he saw a huge castle.

As he got closer, Jack realized the castle must be the home of a giant. The doors were so big, Jack could walk beneath them.

Once inside, Jack wandered into a room where a giant was counting gold coins. Suddenly, the giant looked up and bellowed, "Fee-fi-fo-fum! I smell the blood of an Englishman!" The giant looked around, but didn't see tiny Jack. After a while, the giant left the room.

Jack saw his chance. He snatched a gold coin and ran from the castle. He finally reached the beanstalk, threw the coin down into his mother's garden, and climbed down as fast as he could.

With the gold coin, Jack and his mother bought food and made their house comfortable. But one day, the money ran out. Jack knew that he had to return to the castle.

He climbed back up the beanstalk. This time, he found the giant holding a hen. "Lay!" yelled the giant, and the hen laid a golden egg. When the giant walked away with the egg, leaving the hen behind, Jack grabbed the hen and took it to his mother.

Curious about the giant's treasures, Jack climbed the beanstalk one more time. He found the giant with a tiny harp. "Play!" yelled the giant, and the harp sang a beautiful song. Within minutes, the giant had fallen asleep.

Jack tiptoed over to the harp. Suddenly, in a loud, clear voice, the harp sang out, "Someone is stealing me!"

The giant woke up immediately. "Fee-fi-fo-fum! I see the face of an Englishman!" Jack grabbed the harp and dashed out of the castle. He ran through the clouds to the beanstalk. The harp sang for her life, all the while.

"*Sssshh!* I am rescuing you from the giant," said Jack. Finally, the harp understood. She began to sing a happy song.

With the giant close behind, Jack climbed down the beanstalk. He gave the harp to his mother and picked up an ax. With three mighty swings, Jack chopped down the beanstalk. Jack and his mother never saw the giant again.

With the golden eggs from the hen and the sweet music of the harp, Jack and his mother lived happily ever after.

The Flying Prince

Adapted by Brian Conway
Illustrated by Kathi Ember

Prince Rashar lived in a distant land. He spent each day hunting and exploring the jungle. One day, Prince Rashar saw a large parrot land on a branch above him.

"I am the king of the parrots," it said, proudly.

"How is it that you can talk?" asked the prince.

"Princess Saledra gave me that power," he said.

"Interesting… Where can I find this princess?" Prince Rashar asked.

"You could never find her," Parrot King squawked. "She lives far away, in the city where night becomes day."

Curious, Prince Rashar decided to find Princess Saledra, and rode off into the jungle.

Soon Prince Rashar came upon four trolls having an argument.

"Excuse me," the prince said. "Perhaps I can help."

"Our master left us these four magic things," the trolls answered. "But he did not tell us which of us gets what!"

There was a flying carpet that would take its owner wherever he wished to go. There was a cloth bag that would give its holder anything he wished for. And, there was a magic bowl and a magic stick.

"I can help you decide fairly," said the clever prince. "I will shoot an arrow into the jungle. Whoever returns with the arrow, shall keep all of the magic items."

Prince Rashar shot an arrow into the air, and the trolls dashed into the jungle to find it. While they searched, Prince Rashar took the magic items. He rolled out the carpet and sat down on it.

"Carpet, take me to the city where night becomes day," he said.

The magic carpet zoomed through the air, stopping at last in a faraway city. As night began to fall, the prince went to the palace to call on the princess. When the sun set, the city was dark for a moment. Then a door opened at the roof of the palace. Princess Saledra walked out from her room and stepped across the palace rooftop.

Her beauty shone more brightly than the moon. In an instant, night became day. Prince Rashar could not take his eyes off her.

At that moment, he knew he loved the princess.

Prince Rashar took his bag of wishes and said, "Bag, give me a gift that the princess will love." He reached into the bag and found an exquisite silk shawl that matched the princess's gown exactly.

Later that night, after the princess had gone inside, Prince Rashar asked his magic carpet to take him to the room where Princess Saledra slept. The carpet lifted the prince to the palace roof, and he crept through the door, into the princess's room.

Princess Saledra was sleeping soundly in her bed. The prince set the shawl beside her. He stopped to gaze upon her beautiful face.

Just then, the princess awoke! She was frightened at first, but the prince explained who he was. The princess saw that he was a very handsome man and that he spoke from his heart. Her heart softened further when she saw his gift to her. The princess smiled the brightest smile ever seen.

At that moment, Prince Rashar and Princess Saledra fell in love. They were soon married. And each day forever after, the prince and princess flew over their kingdom on the magic carpet.

Rumpelstiltskin

Adapted by Anne H. Foley
Illustrated by David Hohn

A miller and his daughter once delivered some flour to the king.

To impress the king, the miller boasted, "Your Majesty, my daughter is very special. She can spin ordinary straw into gold!"

"Indeed!" said the greedy king. "She must prove her talent."

The king led the girl to a room filled with straw.

"Spin all of this into gold by tomorrow morning," he said, shutting the door.

But the miller's daughter did not really know how to spin straw into gold. In despair, she began to weep.

Suddenly, a voice asked, "Why are you crying?"

The miller's daughter looked up and saw an odd little man. She explained her dilemma.

"I will spin this straw into gold for you," said the man, "if you give me your necklace."

The miller's daughter agreed, and the man set to work.

The next morning, the king was delighted to see that all the straw had been spun into gold. He led the miller's daughter to another, much larger room filled with straw.

"Spin all of this into gold by tomorrow morning, and you shall become queen," said the king, leaving the room.

"I cannot do it!" she sobbed.

Just then the little man reappeared. "I will do it for you," he said, "if you give me your firstborn child."

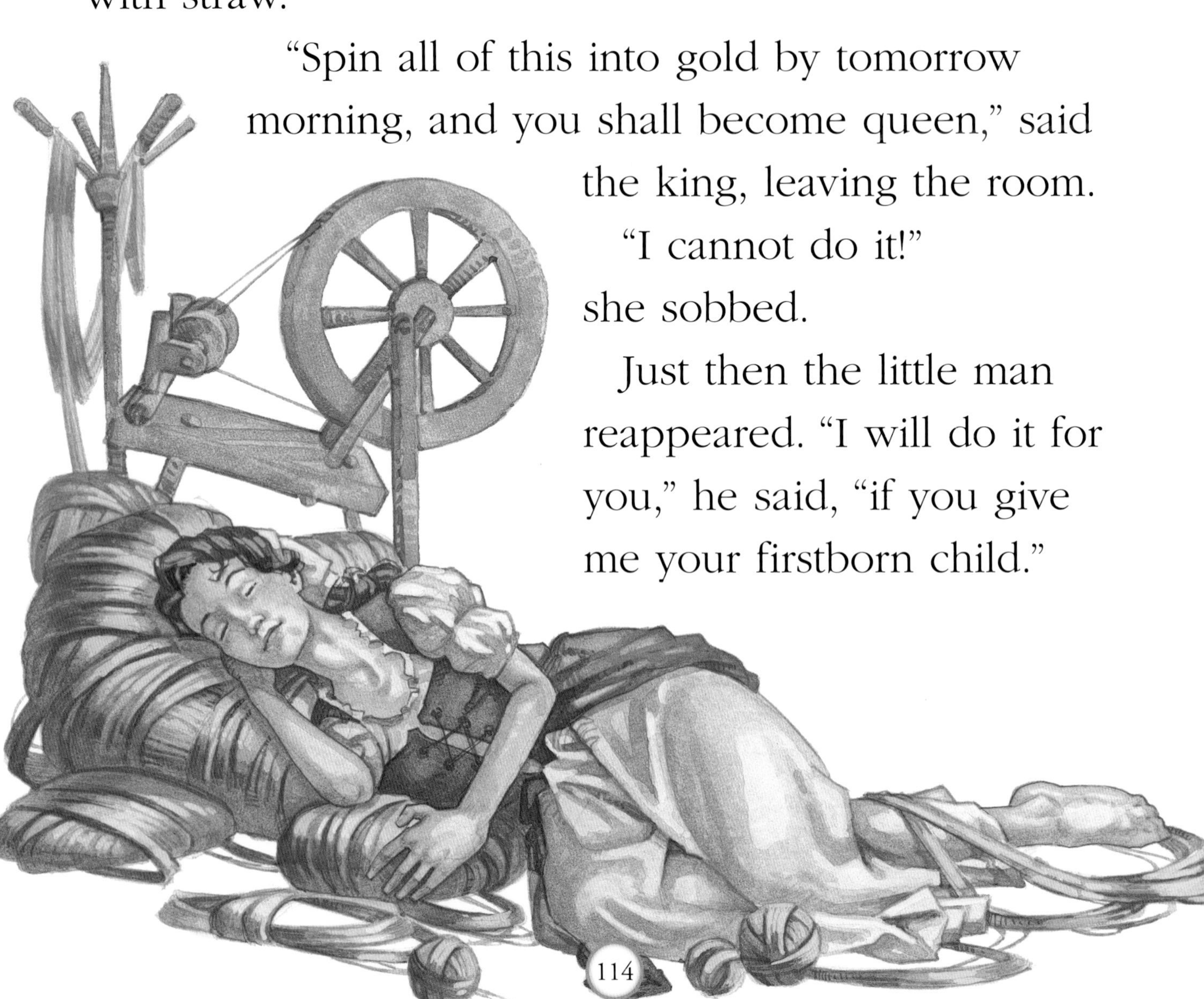

The miller's daughter felt she had no choice, and agreed to the awful request. She slept as the little man worked.

By sunrise, all of the straw had once again been turned to gold.

"You are a woman of incredible skill, and I would like you to be my wife!" cried the king upon seeing the miracle.

The miller's daughter and the king were soon married.

Within a year, the queen gave birth to a daughter. She had forgotten all about her agreement with the little man, until one day when he suddenly appeared.

"I have not forgotten our deal," he said. "Give me your daughter."

"Oh please, do not take my child!" pleaded the desperate queen.

"Very well, I will give you another chance," he said.

"You have three days to guess my name. If you guess correctly, you can keep your baby. But if you cannot guess, I get your child."

The next day, the strange little man arrived to hear the queen's first guesses.

The queen read a long list of names, but not a single one of them was correct.

The queen was very worried. She sent messengers all over the kingdom, telling them to remember every unusual name they heard.

When the little man returned, the queen read a list of all the odd names found by her messengers. But at the end of the second day, she still did not know his name.

On the third day, a messenger came running into the palace.

"Your Majesty, I have seen an odd little man dancing around a fire, singing:

The queen's heart will break,
For her child I'll take.
I'll win the guessing game,
For Rumpelstiltskin is my name!

Soon the little man arrived. The queen looked him in the eye and asked, "Is your name Rumpelstiltskin?"

"How did you know?" screamed the little man, stomping his feet in anger.

He stomped so hard that he kicked a hole right through the floor! In an instant, the strange little man disappeared, never to be seen again.

The Princess and the Pea

Adapted by Lora Kalkman
Illustrated by Carolyn Croll

A handsome prince lived in a faraway land with his parents, the king and queen. More than anything, the prince wanted to get married and have a family of his own.

So he set out to find a special princess to be his bride, traveling to kingdoms far and wide. The prince met many beautiful princesses, all of whom wanted to marry him.

But the prince did not think any of the princesses were special enough.

After his long search, the prince gave up and returned to the castle. The king and queen saw how downhearted their son was and decided to help. They planned a royal ball, inviting all the princesses in the kingdom. All of the princesses wanted to marry the prince. But the prince found something wrong with every one of them.

Three days later, a princess from a distant kingdom was traveling near the prince's castle, when suddenly it began to rain. Thunder crashed and lightning flashed. The storm scared the horses, and the carriage got stuck in the mud.

"What shall we do?" asked the princess's driver. "The horses cannot move the carriage another inch."

The princess was very smart. "I will walk to that castle nearby and ask if we can spend the night," she said. "Surely, they will help us."

Wet from the rain and covered in mud, the princess knocked on the heavy door of the castle. When the prince opened the door, he was stunned at the sight of the girl. The princess explained her plight, and the prince invited her to stay.

The queen asked the servants to fix up a special bed just for the girl. The servants stacked up twenty comfy mattresses and twenty fluffy quilts. Then the queen tucked a tiny green pea underneath the bottom mattress.

"If she is truly a princess," said the queen, "she will not be able to sleep. Only a true princess will be able to feel the hard pea under all these layers."

Exhausted from her journey, the princess climbed a ladder and got into the tall, cozy bed.

But when the princess snuggled in, she did not feel comfortable at all.

This tall bed is awfully lumpy and bumpy, she thought. *It feels like there is a giant rock in the bed!*

Although the princess was very tired, she was not able to sleep. She tossed and turned all night long in the lumpy, bumpy bed.

The next morning, the princess walked to the royal garden to meet the king, queen, and prince for breakfast.

"How did you sleep?" asked the queen.

"Not very well," admitted the princess. "In fact, I couldn't sleep a wink! I found this pea underneath the bottom mattress of my bed." The princess held out the tiny pea for the queen to see.

The queen was delighted. *Only a real princess would feel the pea,* she thought.

Only a special princess could feel the pea, the prince thought, happily. Surely, this was the special princess he had been looking for!

The prince asked the princess to marry him. The king and queen planned a joyful wedding and invited everyone in the kingdom. The prince and princess got married, and everyone lived happily ever after.

Pinocchio

Adapted by Elizabeth Olson
Illustrated by David Austin Clar

One day, an old man named Geppetto saw a bluebird resting on a log. "This log will make your dreams come true," whistled the bird. Geppetto decided to carve a puppet from the wood.

When Geppetto finished, he stepped back to admire his work. "I will call you Pinocchio," he said to the puppet.

With that, Pinocchio stood up and winked at Geppetto. Then he darted out the door!

"Come back!" cried Geppetto.

But Pinocchio kept running. As he ran, his nose began to grow! From then on, whenever he was bad, Pinocchio's nose grew longer.

When a policeman saw the puppet, he grabbed him firmly by the nose. "You should be in school," he said.

"I'd rather play all day!" replied Pinocchio.

Out of breath, old Geppetto appeared and took Pinocchio back home.

Later that day, Gepetto gave Pinocchio two coins to buy a book for school. Pinocchio set off immediately. Soon he came upon two beggars who told Pinocchio that if he buried his money, it would grow into a money tree.

Just then, a bluebird called out, “Don’t be foolish!” But Pinocchio paid no attention.

The cat and fox showed Pinocchio where to bury his money, and told him to go away for a bit to allow the plant to grow.

When Pinocchio returned later, all he found was an empty hole where he had buried the coins. He had been tricked.

Then Pinocchio heard the bird singing overhead again. He looked up to see a beautiful fairy.

"Pinocchio," she said, "if you are good, and if you obey Geppetto, then one day you shall become a real boy!" She swung Pinocchio onto her back and flew him home.

"I promise to be good from now on," said a hopeful Pinocchio.

On his way to school the next day, a man asked Pinocchio where he was going.

"To school," said Pinocchio.

"Why go to school when you can play?" asked the man. "Come with me to Playland."

Just then, a bluebird sang out, "Don't be foolish!" But Pinocchio paid no attention.

"Okay, I'll go," said Pinocchio. And off they went.

One day in Playland, something very surprising happened to Pinocchio. Because he had been bad for so long, he sprouted donkey ears—and a tail as well!

"I don't want to be a donkey. *Hee-haw*," cried Pinocchio.

Pinocchio heard a whistle and looked up to see the fairy. "I will take away your donkey ears and tail, but I cannot take you home," she said. "Your father is not there. He has been searching for you, and he is now lost at sea."

"I will search the sea until I find Gepetto!" said Pinocchio.

After several days of swimming, Pinocchio saw a giant whale. The whale yawned and swallowed Pinocchio! The scared puppet floated down into the whale's stomach.

"Is someone there?" said a quiet voice. A match flared, and Pinocchio saw Geppetto.

"Oh, Father, I have found you!"cried Pinocchio. The two embraced just as the whale's stomach shook violently.

"The whale has the hiccups," said Gepetto. Suddenly, Pinocchio and Geppetto were hiccuped out of the whale. They swam back to the shore.

Pinocchio heard a familiar whistle and looked up to see the bluebird. "Brave Pinocchio," it sang, "all your misdeeds are forgiven. Be a good boy from now on."

At once, Pinocchio felt different. "Look at me, Father!" he said. "I am a real live boy!"

The sight of his son brought tears of joy to Gepetto's eyes.

Beauty and the Beast

Adapted by Amy Adair
Illustrated by David Merrell

There once was a rich man who fell upon hard times. He was forced to move his family to the country, and his children were very unhappy there. But one daughter, Beauty, was always hopeful.

One day, Beauty's father decided to travel to the city to look for work. All the children asked their father to bring them back fine clothes and trinkets, but all Beauty wanted was a single red rose.

Beauty's father reached the city, but could find no work. Saddened, he began the long journey home. On the way, it started to snow so hard he could barely see the trail ahead of him. Suddenly, he felt a warm breeze. He went a little farther and found himself in the middle of a summery garden.

Beauty's father had stumbled upon an enchanted castle. He knocked on the door, but when no one answered, he stepped inside. He walked down a great hall until he found a dining room with a table full of delicious food. He ate his fill, then fell asleep.

The next morning, as he was leaving, he saw a blooming red rosebush. Remembering Beauty's request, he picked a flower.

Suddenly, a horrible beast appeared and growled, "Is this my thanks? I feed and shelter you and then you steal from me?" To repay him for the rose, the beast demanded to be given one of the man's daughters.

Beauty's father returned home and told his children what had happened.

"It was my rose that started the trouble," said Beauty, "so I must be the one to go."

The next day, Beauty arrived at the beast's castle. She saw that the beast's eyes were kind, and she was not afraid.

Beauty quickly made the castle her home. Every night, she dined with the gentle beast. Beauty grew to be quite fond of him.

One night, Beauty asked the beast if she could go home for a visit. The beast agreed that she could go home for two months.

The beast gave Beauty a trunk full of gifts to take to her family. He also gave her a magic ring with a large red jewel. The ring would take her home when she turned it on her finger.

When Beauty magically appeared at home, her family was thrilled to see her. She gave them the trunk full of gifts, and they all marveled at the beast's generosity.

Beauty enjoyed being with her family, but soon she began to miss the beast.

One night, Beauty looked deep into the jewel and saw the beast laying in his garden. He seemed to be dying! Distraught, she turned the ring on her finger and magically returned to the castle.

Beauty rushed to the beast's side. "Oh, please do not die!" she cried. "I never knew it before, but I love you!"

"Will you marry me, Beauty?" the beast whispered.

"Yes," Beauty answered breathlessly.

Suddenly, there was a flash of light and the beast changed into a handsome prince!

"An enchantress put me under an evil spell—only true love could free me," the prince explained. "Your love broke the spell!"

The prince sent for Beauty's family, and he and Beauty were married the next day. They all lived happily ever after in the enchanted castle.

The Elves and the Shoemaker

Adapted by Jennifer Boudart
Illustrated by Kristen Goeters

One harsh winter, a poor shoemaker and his wife discovered that they had only enough leather left to make one pair of shoes. After the leather was gone, they would have no way to make a living, for they could not afford any more.

"Things will work out," said the shoemaker. He cut out the leather and went to bed, planning to finish the shoes the next day.

In the morning, instead of the pieces of leather, the shoemaker found a marvelous pair of shoes! The shoes were beautifully made, with fantastic detail. *Who could have made these?* he wondered, amazed.

That day, a rich tourist came into the shoemaker's shop. "I've stepped in a puddle of sludge, and I simply can't walk around in these muddy shoes," he said. "Do you have anything in my size?"

The shoemaker and his wife showed him the mysterious shoes. They were a perfect fit!

"These are the loveliest shoes I've ever seen!" exclaimed the traveler, giving the shoemaker a shiny gold coin to pay for them.

With the gold coin, the shoemaker bought enough leather to make two pairs of shoes. Once again, the shoemaker cut the leather and placed the pieces on his workbench. The next morning, he found two more pairs of fabulous shoes.

This continued for many nights, until the shoemaker's shelves were filled with beautiful shoes like no one had ever seen before.

Word of the shoemaker's fine shoes soon made him the most popular shoemaker in the land. But still something bothered him. One evening he said to his wife, "Every night, someone works hard to help us. It's a shame we don't even know who it is. Why don't we stay up to find out?"

That night, just like always, the shoemaker cut leather into pieces and placed them on his workbench. But instead of going to bed, he and his wife hid in the doorway.

Soon two elves appeared on the workbench! Their clothes were old and ragged, and they must have been quite cold. Nevertheless, they worked happily all through the night.

"Clearly they are in great need," said the shoemaker, "yet they work all night to help us."

The shoemaker's wife had an idea. "Let's make those little elves the clothes they need!" she said. That evening, instead of leaving leather on the bench, they left tiny new clothes and shoes.

The elves magically appeared at midnight. They climbed upon the workbench and saw the two tiny suits. Their little faces brightened and they shouted gleefully. At once, they put on the fine new suits and shoes. They were so excited they began to dance and sing.

After that night, the elves never came back. But the shoemaker and his wife did not mind. They were just glad they had been able to help. The shoemaker remained successful for the rest of his days, and he and his wife never forgot the kindness of the two little strangers.

Rapunzel

Adapted by Jennifer Boudart
Illustrated by Kathi Ember

A poor couple lived next door to a witch who had a lush garden.

One evening, the wife, who was going to have a baby, said to her husband, "I would love to eat some of the witch's sweet Rapunzel lettuce."

The caring husband crept into the witch's garden. As he picked a head of lettuce, it began to scream!

The witch appeared and said, “Take all the lettuce you want. But in return, you must give me your baby when it is born.”

Terrified, the man ran home. He did not tell his wife what the witch had said. Surely, he could think of a way to break the promise.

The next morning, the wife had a baby girl and named her Rapunzel. The witch came and took the baby that very day.

The witch took Rapunzel to live in a tower in the middle of nowhere. The witch was kind to Rapunzel, and loved her like a daughter. But she would not let Rapunzel leave the tower.

The years passed, and Rapunzel grew to be a lovely young woman with long, shiny golden hair. But she was very lonely. She had never even seen another person besides the witch.

Rapunzel began to wonder about other people. Rapunzel's curiosity worried the witch.

To keep her daughter to herself, the witch put a powerful spell on the tower that sealed the door. To get into the tower, the witch would call out, "Rapunzel, Rapunzel, let down your hair."

Rapunzel would come to the window and unwind her long braids. The witch would grab hold of each braid and climb up to the window.

One morning, a prince was exploring his kingdom when he saw an isolated tower in the distance. Through his telescope, he watched an old woman walk up to the tower and shout, "Rapunzel, Rapunzel, let down your hair."

A beautiful maiden appeared and hung her braids out the window. The old woman used them to climb the tower wall.

Before long, the maiden dropped her braids again, and the old woman climbed back down and disappeared into the woods.

The prince approached the tower. He tried to open the door, but it was sealed tightly shut.

"Rapunzel, Rapunzel, let down your hair," he called.

The maiden unwrapped her hair, and the prince climbed inside the tower.

"Who are you?" he asked.

Rapunzel told the prince her story.

"I can take you away from this tower," said the prince, "and you can be free."

Rapunzel knew this could be her only chance to escape. She let down her hair so the prince could climb down. Then Rapunzel closed her eyes and jumped, landing safely in the prince's arms.

As they rode away, Rapunzel and the prince talked and talked.

Rapunzel was delighted to speak to someone other than the witch. When they came to a little village, they passed a shack where an old man and woman were working in their garden. When they overheard the prince call the girl Rapunzel, they looked at each other. Instantly, they knew that this must be their long-lost daughter, and they called out to the prince to stop.

And so, after many years, the family was finally reunited. They lived in happiness together, forever after.

The End